Gumbles on

S. A. Wakefield lives with his wife on a small farm, about fifty miles north of Sydney. He loves the Australian bush and his feelings for it, coupled with a wonderful sense of fun and fantasy, bubble forth in the hilarious adventures of the scaly Bottersnikes and the squashy Gumbles.

Desmond Digby's beautifully witty illustrations mirror the imaginative quality of Sam Wakefield's text. Like the author, Desmond Digby has a great affection for the Australian landscape. Born in New Zealand, he has a high reputation as a stage designer and satiric painter. His drawings are beautifully executed, with an eye for the small details in which children delight.

S. A. Wakefield

Gumbles on Guard

Illustrated by

Desmond Digby

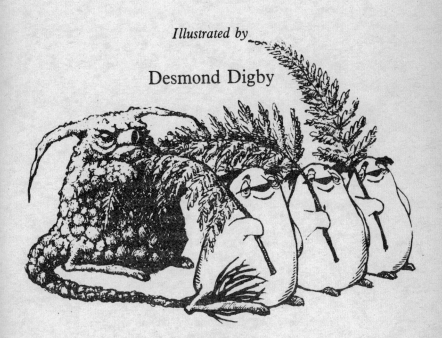

Piccolo Books

For Betty

First published 1975 by William Collins Pty Ltd, Sydney
This Piccolo edition published 1984 by Pan Books Ltd,
Cavaye Place, London SW10 9PG
Text © S. A. Wakefield 1975
Illustrations © Desmond Digby 1975
ISBN 0 330 28192 5
Phototypeset by Input Typesetting Ltd, London
Printed and bound in Great Britain by
Cox & Wyman Ltd, Reading

CONTENTS

CHAPTER ONE

Supergumble

'Lyrebird will not come,' Happigumble said, 'unless you stop giggling, Willigumble, and making such a noise.'

It is hard for any Gumble to keep still and quiet, and for Willigumble hardest of all; but this is what they must do, Happigumble explained, if they wanted to see Lyrebird dance and display his tail. 'Everything must be right for him or he will not come. Lyrebird is very fussy.'

'I have heard him sing,' Willigumble said. 'He just copies other birds.'

'Wait till you have seen him dance! There is nothing like it in the whole bush. Not in the whole of Australia.'

'Well I hope he hurries,' Willigumble said.

All around them, great trees towered toward the sun. In their shade smaller bushes grew and tangles of vines, and beneath these a forest of graceful fern, each frond like an umbrella for the Gumbles, who are only small. With his own claws Lyrebird had scratched a small clearing to dance on, and by the edge of this the Gumbles waited, hiding, almost drowning in the green of ferns.

When at last he came Lyrebird did not fly but came on foot, through a tunnel in the green. He was a brown bird about the size of a hen. Not handsome: his colours were drab, his feet huge, his tail an untidy draggle brushing the ground behind him. But he could sing! He knew all the songs of the bush birds and he could copy three or four kookaburras laughing together, or the squawks of a whole flock of parrots and the rustle of their wings as well. All from the throat of a plain brown bird standing cocked on his mound, like an actor centre-stage. Then he stopped singing and lowered his head, scratched earth, shook out his tail like a fan, and the plain brown bird vanished into a shower of feathers, shimmering and silvery and swaying; so magical that when the silverdance was over the Gumbles could not stop themselves bursting into claps and cheers.

'I knew you were watching!' Lyrebird said, though he looked startled.

'More! More! Encore!' the Gumbles cried.

'That's all very well,' Lyrebird said rather pettishly. 'I have to be in the mood. It takes a lot out of a chap.'

'If I could sing and dance like that I'd do it all day long!' Willigumble shouted. 'Lyrebird. . . .' Then, in the presence of a genuine artist, he became shy.

'What is it, Willigumble?'

'Did it take you long to learn?' he whispered.

Everyone laughed, but Willi was quite serious about it. 'You had to learn when you were little, didn't you? Well, I'm little and I want to learn.'

A bright clear *tink* came from somewhere in the fern. Lyrebird cocked his ear at once. 'That's an interesting sound! Who made it?'

'Me,' said Tinkingumble. 'It pops out when I get a good idea, I can't help it. I thought, if there is a lyrebird chick this year Willi could take dancing lessons with him. I only meant it as a joke.'

'It's a good idea!' cried Willi, jumping. 'Tink's tinks are always good. *Is* there a chick this year?' — for the mother lyrebird, Willi knew, laid only one egg a season.

'Oh I expect so,' Lyrebird said. 'The wife has been fussing for some weeks. Nesting. Brooding. In the usual way.'

'You never help her,' Happigumble remarked. Most of the birds the Gumbles knew helped their mates at nesting time, either with the building or keeping the eggs warm, or finding food for the chicks. Lyrebird never did.

'Nests! Eggs! That sort of thing is not for me. My tail,' Lyrebird said, sweeping it over his head and shimmering grandly, 'would never fit in any nest. Now would it?'

'He's a Superbird!' Willigumble squeaked, in admiration of that wonderful tail.

'But he won't help with the nesting. He could find worms for the chick without spoiling his precious tail,' Happigumble whispered.

'Winter's my busy season!' Lyrebird said. 'Concerts to give, dances to do! And I have nine mounds to keep in order — kindly leave this one tidy when you go — now how can I find time for worms?' He scratched fussily at his mound, which was already tilled well enough to grow beans, and ran briskly into the fern. 'You'll find the wife's nest at the bottom of the cliff somewhere,' he called back. 'Unless she changed her mind.'

In a moment or two, from his next mound, they heard his strong voice trying out the new sound he had picked up from

Tinkigumble. 'Tink. tink. Tink! *Tink!*'

Tinkigumble held his hands over his ears. 'I wish he wouldn't! He is filling my head with ideas that aren't there.'

'He is a wonderful mimic and a wonderful dancer,' Merrigumble said, 'but he is not a good husband.'

'I am going to learn to sing and dance like Lyrebird,' Willigumble announced. 'I am going to be a Supergumble.' For a tail he plucked a frond of fern to hold behind him and managed a comical shuffle of a dance on Lyrebird's mound, with the fern drooping over his head; but he was not as skilful as the Superbird and his voice was squeaky.

'Not bad for a beginner, Willi,' he was told, 'though you have a lot to learn.'

'Then we'll find the mother Lyrebird's nest and see when the chick is going to start lessons,' he said. 'I *will* be a Supergumble! I'll practise every day.'

'Wait! Someone's coming,' said Happigumble.

Near them the fern fronds were swaying, moved by something bigger than Lyrebird, something padding very quietly. A gleam of chestnut red showed through the fern. Fox! Fox had no friends in the bush. He was very cunning, and a clever hunter; sometimes he killed for sport. So the Gumbles froze into the fern, and in the middle of the mound little Willi wished that his shimmery fern frond was a great tree to hide him. The Gumbles were not afraid of being eaten.

Though plump, they are too squashy for the taste of meat-eaters. The peculiar thing about them is that they can be stretched or squeezed to any shape without hurting, and if squeezed hard they cannot pop back to their proper Gumbleshapes unless helped. Nearly all the bush creatures are friendly with the squashy, cheerful Gumbles. Fox was different. They never trusted Fox, never made friends.

Fox stepped on to the mound and turned his sharp face into the fern, as if he knew the Gumbles were hiding there. Willi tried to stand motionless but his tail-fern shivered from fright. Fox sniffed him all over, paused a moment, then walked unhurriedly away.

The Gumbles rushed to Willi, dusted him and fussed. He was all right, though, apart from being a little shaky. 'Grasshoppers! I never want that to happen again! I thought he was going to bite my head off.'

'Lucky Willi's a Gumble and not a real lyrebird chick!'

'But if there is a lyrebird chick,' Happigumble said slowly, 'Fox might have eaten it already.'

When he was hungry, the Gumbles knew, Fox ate almost anything he could catch.

'My dancing lessons!' squeaked Willi. 'Quick! We must find that nest and see if everything's all right.'

Near the edge of the dense bush a cliff of grey rocks rose, carved and hollowed by weather into smooth shapes and shallow caves. The Gumbles searched along the foot of it, clambering boulders and fallen logs, and presently they found the lyrebird's nest, high up, concealed beneath an overhanging rock. To reach it they crept along a ledge until they were standing in the little yellow cave where the nest was, roofed and weatherproofed with fern stems and moss, the opening facing outwards.

Willigumble put his head in and called, 'Anyone home?' and pulled it out again rather quickly. 'There *is* a lyrebird chick! And he's the ugliest thing I've ever seen. He's all beak and squawk and hardly any feathers.'

'He will be all right when he grows,' Willi was told.

'I don't want dancing lessons with a thing like that! He is as ugly as a Bottersnike. Nearly.'

A shrill 'chip chip' came from inside the nest, angry, or alarmed, or both.

12

'He can't even sing yet!' Willigumble said.

At the sound of her chick's cry the mother lyrebird arrived almost at once with a beakful of worms, half flying, half bounding from the ground below. She was not alarmed at seeing her visitors were Gumbles, and when she had stuffed the worms into her little monster's gaping beak she was able to say: 'Isn't he beautiful? Isn't he just like his pa?'

'He hasn't got any feathers much,' Willigumble complained.

'And might be cold when the winds blow,' Happigumble added quickly.

'He will not!' the mother said. 'I have lined the nest with feathers of my own.'

Willigumble asked, not quite so eagerly now: 'Are you going to teach him to sing and dance?'

'Sing and dance! We have no time for those capers, baby and me.' From a small pouch in her throat Lyrebird produced more food which the chick gobbled in a second. 'We have such a lot of growing to do first, haven't we? But there is nothing wrong with our appetite.'

'Speaking of appetites,' said Happigumble gravely, 'we've bad news. Fox is back.'

This did not seem to worry the mother at all. Tinkingumble

13

explained: 'What we're afraid of is that while you're away finding worms Fox might climb the ledge, like we did, and . . . raid the nest,' *and gobble up that chick, chip and all,* they thought, but did not say, *which would be very sad, because though he is a little monster now he will grow into a beautiful dancer, and the world needs beautiful things.*

'Chip chip!' went the chick loudly.

'Still hungry!' the mother said. And she looked tired. 'Isn't he the bonny boy, with the best appetite you ever saw?' She glided to the ground, rather clumsily because her tail, which was her rudder, was bent from long hours of brooding in the nest.

'It is not safe to leave Chip-Chip alone. Not with Fox around,' Happigumble said anxiously.

'What can she do?' said Tinkingumble. 'She must go away to find worms for that huge appetite of his.'

'It is a pity the father won't help. One of them could find food while the other guarded the nest, if he wasn't all the time singing and dancing.'

'But he is a Superbird,' Willigumble said stoutly. 'And I'm going to be a Supergumble.'

Happigumble decided for them all, as he often did. 'There is only one thing for it. *We* shall have to guard the nest. Until Chip-Chip is fledged or until Fox goes away. No fun and games for a while! We've got an important job to do,' and they put their heads together to decide how the nest should be guarded from that cunning enemy, Fox.

Willigumble sighed. Guard duty over an ugly chick, while it squeaked and gobbled worms and slowly slowly grew its feathers, was not his idea of fun for a young Supergumble. But what the others did Willi did too, though he made fun and games of it wherever he could; and when he saw a piece of string that happened to be dangling by the mouth of the cave he jumped to reach it, and discovered that he could

14

swing *whee up*, *whee back*, over the heads of the others as they seriously discussed Fox.

'. . . too high for him to jump,' Happigumble was saying, 'so Chip-Chip would be quite safe if we can stop Fox climbing up the ledge. Now how do we do that?' Plenty of ideas popped up. Build a barricade! Pelt him with rocks! *Tink*, make the ledge slippery! Build a barrier of brambles! Make a booby trap of stones to fall on him!

'Chip-Chip's nest will be as safe as a bank, ho ho!' Tinkingumble chuckled, 'with us on the job.'

'And while we're on the job we're not going to get caught by the Bottersnikes,' Happigumble said. 'Do you hear? Everyone must be extra careful.'

'We always are!'

'Let's get busy then. You too, Willi. Willigumble? Willigumble! Where's he gone, bother his head?'

'Here's a string,' said Tink. 'Perhaps he climbed up. Thinking he was a Supergumble.'

They looked at the string, and wondered. Why should it be there, so close to the nest? What was at the other end of it? From the cave these puzzles could not be answered. Recognizing a ball of fur high in a nearby tree as one of their friends, they yelled: 'Hey, Koala! Can you see where that string comes from?'

'Yairs,' said Koala sleepily.

The Gumbles tried not to sound impatient — Koala was a slow fellow, not to be hurried.

'Tell us about it, Koala.'

'A . . . creature . . . is holding the end. On the cliff top, right over your heads.'

'What sort of a creature?'

'A fat thing . . . ungoodlooking,' Koala said slowly, like a critic trying to be fair, 'in fact, as ugly as a lump. It has knobbles all over . . . a bad cheese for a face . . . and its tail, you wouldn't read about it.'

'Long red ears?' the Gumbles asked.

'Yairs. There are lots of them, all over the rock.'

'Bottersnikes!' the Gumbles groaned. 'Wouldn't it? Just when we have this important job to do.'

'And they've caught Willi already, I suppose,' said Tink gloomily.

Koala had seen the whole misfortune happen. It began with a rumpus in the bushes up there, leaves trembling, branches splitting, as though a small earthquake was on its way. Bottersnikes hate the bush, hate bushwalking, and do whatever damage they can as they waddle through it. As they crashed out of the scrub on to the flat rocks of the cliff top Koala saw that their ears glowed bright red from anger. They were hunting Gumbles and had found none. Their rusty jam tins, which they had brought to put the Gumbles in when captured, contained nothing. Besides being angry about this they were very tired, for Bottersnikes are most likely the laziest creatures in the world, or anywhere.

A particularly fat one, who was being carried by two others, came to the edge of the cliff and stared at the miles and miles of treetops that could be seen from that height.

'It is like a sea,' the King of the Bottersnikes declared.

Nobody argued.

'Where there is sea there will be fish,' the King announced. 'Give me a fishing line.'

Amongst some rubbish lying near the cliff top a length of string was found. This was tied to a stick and given to his majesty, who threw out with a royal gesture, not bothering about bait. As his line chanced to drop outside the cave where

17

the Gumbles were, the King made a catch almost immediately
— Willigumble. The King accepted this piece of good luck
as due to his skill as a fisherman.

'Got you!' he shouted triumphantly, and grabbed Willi off
the line and squashed him into a jam tin. Flattened like dough
in the tin, Willi had no chance of escape.

The other Bottersnikes gathered round to peer and poke at
the King's catch. Being too lazy to look after themselves,
nothing pleases them more than capturing Gumbles as slaves.
One Gumble, however, is not much use to the whole band,
and the King announced: 'I shall now catch the rest and we
shall get some work done.'

After a full minute with no luck the King of the Bottersnikes lost his temper and said: 'They are there, the Gumbles.
I can hear 'em chatterin'. Someone must go down and make
'em bite.'

The Bottersnikes blinked at this for the cliff was forty feet
high and perilous. The King insisted: 'Someone must go!
Smiggles. Wake him up.'

Smiggles, the dreamer, had just drifted into a peaceful doze
on the rock. Often it was as well to keep him awake; some of
his dreams were disasters. So the unlucky Smiggles was
kicked and jumped on till he woke and with a plastic clothes

line tied to his tail pushed over the edge and lowered.

'Great horny dragons!' the Gumbles cried, scrambling to the back of the cave, 'They are coming after us.' They found it quite easy to avoid Smiggles, who could only snatch at air whilst dangling on his rope, but they could not prevent him seeing the lyrebird's nest as he swung to and fro and — worse — could not stop him looking in. Smiggles too had never beheld anything as ugly as the chick, having never owned a mirror; he gave a shriek and yelled to be hauled up.

'Make those fish bite!' the King ordered sternly.

'There is a monster down here!' Smiggles howled. 'Snapping at me.'

Slowly, Smiggles was hauled up to face the angry King.

'A monster that went *chip chip*,' Smiggles repeated. 'In a nest. It had black beady eyes that looked at me.'

Smiggles was a bit simple, everyone knew; but having a monster down there made the King nervous of more fishing. He ordered two heavy Bottersnikes to sit on Smiggles' head and gave the fishing rod to Chank, with instructions to catch the rest.

Chank liked to think that his ideas were always better than the King's. 'Fishin'!' he said scornfully. 'You'll never ever catch the Gumbles that way.'

'I caught one,' the King snapped. 'You ain't caught any.'

'A small one,' Chank sneered. 'The smallest of the lot. The one they call Willigumble.'

'But I'm going to be a Supergumble,' said Willi, still cheeky though squashed up, 'and then you'd better watch out.'

Most of the Bottersnikes snuffled their noses loudly at this, which meant they thought it funny. Not Chank. Willigumble's boast had given him an idea. Having a smart idea always made Chank as pompous as a big drum. 'Sending Smiggles down's no good. What you want here,' he said grandly, 'is brain. Which is what I got enough to fill a bag with, while with what Smig's got you couldn't raise a blister. Now brain tells me it's easier for the Gumbles to come up than us to go down; and come up is what I shall make 'em do, by hollerin' and shoutin'. You lot join in.' Chank began his hollering and shouting: this he did so well that the Gumbles below had no difficulty in hearing every sound of the fearful racket.

'Having a fight!' the Gumbles said happily. 'When they've worn themselves out we'll go and rescue Willi.'

'Yow-waow! Stop it, stop it!' yelled the voice up top. 'Please, Willigumble! Stop belting me!'

The Gumbles' ears tingled.

'No no, Willi! I can't stand any more!' Another Bottersnike voice joined in: 'Not me, Willigumble, not me! I ain't done nothing!' — and soon they were all at it: 'Don't hit me, Willigumble, *please* Willigumble, let me alone — cor! What a terror he is!'

The Gumbles looked at each other in astonishment. Had Willi actually become a Supergumble, so soon?

'This we have got to see,' they cried. 'Hey, Lyrebird' — who just then arrived with worms — 'look after Chip-Chip for a minute, will you? We must see what's got into Willi.'

Up the cliff they scrambled, scaling it like mountaineers first till they reached a higher ledge, then by making them-

selves a Gumblerope which lassoed the stump of a tree growing in a crevice; up the crevice, panting now, and over the
last rise by spring-and-jump to the very top . . . where groan-
ing 'snikes sprawled on the rocks, flattened; in the middle
one little rusty jam tin standing.

'Willigumble?' they whispered, awestruck by the damage
done.

The tin rattled slightly on the rock as Willigumble's voice
tried to get out — too squashed-up though to sound a proper
warning: 'Careful! It's a trap ——'

'Got you!' the Bottersnikes shouted, and leaping fighting-
fit from the rocks they grabbed the Gumbles and squashed
them into jam tins.

'I knew it'd work! I knew it'd work!' Chank crowed. 'The
Gumbles are curious, see, they were bound to come; fishin's
no good, what you want is brains.' Chank nearly burst with
self importance swaggering there on the cliff, and forty feet
below him the lyrebird chick said 'Chip!' as his mother went
for worms.

CHAPTER TWO

The Palace-mobile

'Now we've got the Gumbles back we can move on and find a better place to live,' Chank said, shuddering at the splendid view from the cliff top.

In front of him mile upon mile of hills stretched to the distant sea. Thousands and thousands of trees. There was no show of life apart from a crow in the sky. Chank shuddered at what he saw. Old stony ridges, lizard-runs, sun-dried and windworn. Deep gullies between, the invisible streams winding. And trees everywhere, patchy green, undisturbed. Clock time might never have begun among those thousands of silent trees.

The cliff on which Chank stood had once been a lookout where people drove in with picnics and cameras. Since then the road had been changed and cars no longer came, bushes grew up thick and prickly beside the entrance, and someone had stolen the safety fence, so that you could walk over the edge if you wanted and fall into Lyrebird's fernbed; and the only visitors to the lookout now were folk who found it a handy dump for their rubbish.

The Bottersnikes were not in the least pleased with the view, which to their way of thinking let in too much cold wind. The rubbish was what they found attractive. Being too lazy to build homes of their own Bottersnikes choose to live in rubbish dumps. Here they laze and sleep, never moving far — especially in rainy weather, for Bottersnikes shrink when wet.

'And the rubbish here is nothing fancy, nothing fancy at all,' Chank grumbled. 'I say we oughta move on to a better-class area.'

But Bottersnikes seldom move unless they must. The King had found an oil drum with the ends missing that suited him perfectly as a palace.

Chank was not happy about the cliff either. 'It is dangerous without a fence. Someone's going to fall over. You're supposed to be the boss,' he said to the King. 'What you going to do about it?'

'Have a feed,' the King said. 'Send them Gumbles to get it ready.'

Half the Gumbles were kept as hostages, half were taken from the tins and sent foraging. Fried mattress stuffing is what Bottersnikes like to eat, and pictures of food cut from magazines (tastier if coloured), and for sweets, bottle tops are favourites.

The Gumbles in the foraging party, once they were out of sight, sat down in a hollow red gum to talk things over. Mountains of 'snikefood lay around them — mattresses, old papers, bottles; and they had to be careful of their feet as a bag of rusty nails had burst open there.

'I'm worried about Chip-Chip,' Tootngumble said.

'I think Chank is right,' said Merrigumble. 'The Bottersnikes should move on. If they stay they will be fighting and falling over and will disturb the lyrebirds.'

'And on the move there should be a chance to escape, all of us,' Jolligumble put in eagerly. 'You know how they crash about in the bush like hippopotamuses. Surely we could slip away and get back to the job of guarding Chip-Chip.'

'But they will put us in jam tins,' said Merrigumble. 'They always do.'

Tootngumble sighed. 'I wish we had Tinkingumble here. His tinks are so bright.' Tink was one of the hostages.

'No one else feels like having a tink, I suppose?'

'Sorry, I only toot. I know it's not much use.'

'Well, some are tinkers and some aren't,' Merrigumble said. 'The thing is to do your best with what you've got, whether it's a tink or a toot. So let's hope the Bottersnikes move on, and that they don't put us in tins, and that we can all escape——'

'And that Fox hasn't eaten Chip-Chip.'

It seemed rather a lot to hope for.

'But it's the best we can do,' said Toot. 'One thing we *won't* do, we won't find them much to eat. Right?'

So when there was a bawling and a howling and a banging of tins for dinner, the foraging party returned with nothing more than a few earwigs in old cardboard boxes — very poor fare for Bottersnikes, especially as the cardboard was bleached and soggy and had lost its taste.

'This sort of tucker ain't for a stewed rabbit!' Chank

25

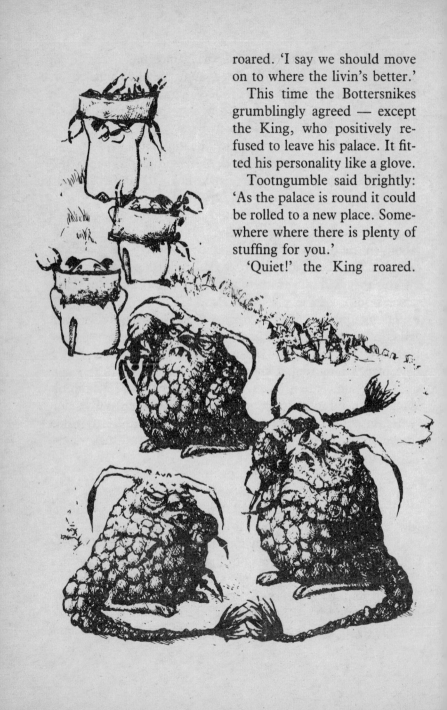

roared. 'I say we should move on to where the livin's better.'

This time the Bottersnikes grumblingly agreed — except the King, who positively refused to leave his palace. It fitted his personality like a glove.

Tootngumble said brightly: 'As the palace is round it could be rolled to a new place. Somewhere where there is plenty of stuffing for you.'

'Quiet!' the King roared.

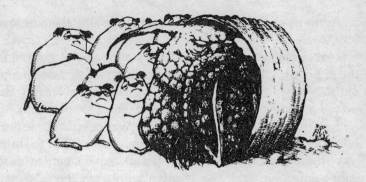

'Gumbles do what they're told. I do the telling. And tin those Gumbles, hard, before they escape.'

It did not seem a good beginning. Nevertheless Tootngumble had started an idea wriggling in the King's mind. He squeezed out of the palace and waddled round it, looking from all angles; he gave it a careful push with his foot and observed that it rolled easily on the flat rock. 'As my palace is round,' the King said thoughtfully, 'it could be rolled to a new place. Somewhere where there is plenty of stuffing for us.'

'Clever, to think of that!' the Bottersnikes admired.

'Because it is a moving palace,' the King explained, to make the why of it exactly clear. 'It is a palace-mobile.'

'And you don't see many of those!' the Bottersnikes said, impressed.

Two strong and sensible 'snikes would see to the rolling, the King said; they were to slow down round corners and not scratch the rust. Glob and Snorg appointed themselves palace-rollers, mainly to keep Chank out of the job.

'Jam tins ready!' roared the King. 'We will travel.' Instead of beginning to waddle *left foot flop! right foot flop!* in the usual way, the King climbed into the palace-mobile, settled down with a snort and said: 'Wake me when we get there.'

Glob and Snorg saw that with his majesty in residence the palace-rolling was going to be hard, hot and heavy. 'Gumbles' work,' Glob growled. 'Why else do we keep the little blighters for?'

'Why should we carry 'em around in tins? Let the little perishers earn their keep,' Snorg said indignantly.

So, as Merrigumble had hoped, the Gumbles were taken from their tins and given orders to roll the palace to where there were mountains of mattress stuffing, with no mucking up on the way.

The move began. Chank and Glob led, each trying to waddle more importantly than the other; next, the palace, pushed by the Gumbles, the King snoring inside and his tail flop-

flopping at each turn; Bottersnikes to right and left, watching for any hanky-panky; more Bottersnikes behind shouting at the Gumbles all the time.

The move stopped almost as soon as it began, when the leaders found their way barred by an animal they had not seen before.

'Out of the way, you idiot dog,'

'Move over, you rotten great cat,' said Chank and Glob together.

The Gumbles peered round the palace to see what strange creature this might be: neither a dog nor a cat — horrors! it was Fox.

'Moving, I see,' said Fox smoothly. 'How I wish I could move as easily. You see, I am lame.'

He wasn't lame when we saw him in the fern, the Gumbles thought.

. 'A rusty nail in my foot,' Fox sounded brave about it. 'Painful! But there.'

The Bottersnikes fell over themselves to be sympathetic — next to bottle tops, rusty nails are their favourite sweets. Fox would not allow his foot to be touched, and bared his teeth when they tried to pull the nail out. It made the Bottersnikes red-eared. The King woke, displeased too. 'We ain't got anywhere, why have we stopped rolling?'

'He's got a nail,' the Bottersnikes explained. 'It's no good to him but he won't let us have it. What a selfish animal he is.' For a moment the attention of the whole grumbling band was fixed on Fox — his injured paw, his particularly sharp teeth.

'Just what we wanted!' Merrigumble whispered. 'They have forgotten us completely.'

It looked like being one of the easiest escapes they had ever had. They put a stone behind the palace to stop it rolling backwards and without any fuss began slipping toward the bush.

'No, no, I shall put up with the nail,' said Fox heroically. 'It is just one of those things. By the way, those squashy little creatures you have with you are nipping off to the scrub. Does that matter?'

'Ho, are they just! *Got you!*' the Bottersnikes yelled, whirling and pouncing in the nick of time to prevent the easiest escape ever. 'Get behind that palace and stay there, ready for when we want to move on.'

'Fox is a clever and useful animal,' the King said, clambering out of his palace. 'We should take him along to guard the Gumbles.'

'We could help each other a lot,' Fox said craftily. 'A lone animal is not safe nowadays. There is a whole bagful of these dangerous nails, spilled——'

'Where? Where?' the Bottersnikes clamoured.

Fox looked at them very coolly. 'Life in the bush isn't easy at the best of times and for a hunter with an injured paw it's very hard indeed. Now if I tell you where the nails are how can you help me find a meal?'

'There is plenty of cardboard,' said Glob.

'He don't eat cardboard, stupid,' said Chank.

'Then what do he eat, fathead?'

'Anything meaty. Or eggy. Almost anything with some

blood in it,' Fox said, licking his lips. 'Not snakes or lizards. Birds are all right. Birds are delicious, especially if young.'

'I'll save you all the birds I catch,' Glob promised. He leapt energetically, quite two inches from the rock, to show the slick catcher he could be.

'You don't have to be able to fly,' Fox remarked. 'Sometimes you have the luck to find them in a nest.'

'Hang on!' said Chank. 'That monster that Smiggles saw. He said it was in a nest.'

During this conversation the Gumbles had been growing more and more dismayed. At the mention of Smiggles' monster they couldn't stand it any longer. 'We've got to do something!' Happigumble burst out. 'And quickly! Tink, can you——?'

But no tink happened to be ready. 'I can't think of anything with Fox looking at me like that,' Tink said.

'Keep those jabbering Gumbles quiet,' the King ordered. 'Smiggles! Come here. Show the nice Fox where your monster is, Smig my boy, and he'll tell us where the nails are, then we'll all have a party with my nails.'

'I ain't going down that cliff again!' Smiggles protested.

'No need,' said Fox quickly. 'Just show me.'

On the dizzy edge of the cliff Smiggles closed his eyes and pointed. Without a word Fox walked along the edge to find a place where the descent was easier. Very soon he reappeared below them, looked up with his sharp and hungry face. The King bellowed directions from the top: 'Walk along that ledge. It'll be easy. Now where are them nails?'

Fox jumped to the ledge. There seemed nothing wrong with his paw from the lithe way he moved. 'I see it — a lyrebird's nest! I have not eaten lyrebird before. It will be a treat.'

'We ain't eaten neither,' the King yelled. 'Where are them nails?'

Fox liked silence for his stealthy hunting. He told them: 'The nails are near a big red gum, you can't miss it,' hoping this would keep them quiet. Unfortunately the Bottersnikes could not tell a red gum from a dandelion. 'Come and show us,' the King yelled.

Fox crawled slowly along the ledge. He thought he could see something in the nest. He thought he could see its eyes.

'Our Chip-Chip,' the Gumbles moaned. The chick with a busy mother and a dancing father. They were almost at their wits' end. What could they do? Even if they escaped they would never get to the nest in time. In desperation they held Tinkingumble upside down, which sometimes helped his tinks to come. It was nearly too late. But with  a sound like a pebble dropping in a deep well it came — a real beauty. 'The palace-mobile!' Tink said.

All he had to do was take the stone from behind it then stand back and pretend that what followed was nothing to do with him. The King's winter residence rolled over the rock, slowly at first, gathering speed . . . it bounced once and trundled over the edge, clattering. The Gumbles never knew if the falling palace actually hit Fox. One thing was certain, it alarmed him very much; Fox yelped, fell or jumped from the narrow ledge and bounded away into the fern. The angry Bottersnikes yelled after him, wanting to know what a red gum was. The Gumbles raised a cheer. Never knowing how close he had come to being a meal himself, Chip-Chip called for dinner.

CHAPTER THREE

One Good Turn Deserves Another

The King of the Bottersnikes was not in the least pleased with the way things had fallen out. Not long ago at a birthday party he had swallowed one of his presents — a whistle; and whenever his rage mounted to danger level the swallowed whistle blew *freep-freep* from the depths of the royal stomach. Now the King stood on the cliff top with his stomach whistling shrilly and his ears glowing like August sunsets; he might have crushed the rock to gravel, the way he stamped it in his temper.

'Someone must go down, instantly, and bring my palace back. *Smiggles!*'

'I ain't going down that cliff again!' howled Smiggles. 'Send the Gumbles.'

The King loudly declared that those slippery little beggars couldn't be trusted, what this job needed was an experienced cliff hanger who'd been down before. 'Like Smiggles,' the Bottersnikes agreed, happy not to be doing it themselves. 'Trust old Smig to do a job proper! You Gumbles, find something to let him down on.'

The Gumbles found a plastic clothes line in the rubbish, thrown away because it was frayed in the middle. This they tied to the climber's tail. Glob and Snorg helped him over the edge with a shove while the Gumbles lowered away according to the King's directions. Half way down the rope broke. Smiggles dropped with a shriek, rolled over in the fern and lay like mutton. A peaceful look spread over his face and he failed to stir even when stones they threw landed near.

The King's stomach shrilled again. Sparks shot from his ears. 'Who was the idiot who thought of sending Smiggles down?'

'A bat-eyed bungler, Smiggles,' the Bottersnikes agreed hastily. 'Couldn't fall out of bed without breaking his neck.' However, none of them was smart enough to do what Smiggles could not. They yawned and blinked and scratched, and had nothing better to suggest than sending the Gumbles down.

'Half the Gumbles will go,' the King corrected. It was the turn of Happigumble and those who had been hostages before. 'You're the bottom lot,' the King told them. 'Fasten more rope to my palace and the top lot will pull it up. Any mucking about down there and I'll grind the top lot into putty.'

Very business-like the bottom lot slid down the rope.

The palace had rolled some way down the slope beneath the cliff, out of sight of the Bottersnikes. The Gumbles gathered round it, sized it up and poked it, and stood looking, like men working for pay. 'It would be easier if the King fell over too, and came to live here,' they thought.

A small cry of distress sounded from somewhere in the fern. They forgot the palace at once.

'Gumbles here! Who wants help?'

'Me!' cried a little voice.

'Where are you?'

'Here!'

'Here', they found after a bit of a search, was a deep hole in the ground, 'me' was a very young wallaby that had fallen in. Its mother came thumping through the fern. 'So naughty of him!' she flustered. 'He will not stay in the pouch. This is what happens! He will starve down there.'

'Not to worry,' the Gumbles told her cheerfully. 'We'll have him out in a jiffy.'

The sides and bottom of the hole were slippery with wet white clay. There was nowhere to fasten a Gumblerope, and Joey's legs were the wrong shape to climb ladders. So it needed working out. Tinkingumble hit on the solution with a bright clear tink, about the highest G on the treble clef: 'The palace! Why don't we roll it in? When they pull from the top, up will come palace and Joey and all.'

'Tink's ideas always work, usually!' Willigumble said.

Everything was fixed up at last: the rope attached, the palace lowered into the pit, Joey hopped in. He did not like it and several Gumbles had to jump into the clay to coax him. When he was safely aboard Happigumble sang out 'Haul away!' and from then on the tink worked very well indeed. Up came the palace, out of the pit — Joey was saved. They wiped him down a bit and he dived head first into his mother's pouch, somersaulted in there and stuck his head out, happy now.

'If I can ever do you Gumbles a good turn,' the relieved mother said, 'I hope you will let me know.'

As the palace was being hauled up the cliff — a slow job, for the top lot were not trying hard — Happigumble had time to visit the lyrebird's nest to see if everything was all right.

'Perfectly all right!' he was told. 'Every day we get better and better, baby and me. And such lots of worms we eat.'

'That's fine, then,' said Happigumble, deciding not to tell her about Fox's unsuccessful raid. 'Well, don't worry about a thing. We'll be keeping an eye on you.' All the same I don't like it, he thought as he rejoined the others. Fox knows where the nest is and so do the Bottersnikes and — O, grasshoppers, I hope Tink comes up with something.

Presently the King had his palace again, delivered safe and sound to the top of the cliff, but he was not pleased. During the rescue it had been dolloped and daubed with white clay, printed inside and out with the Gumbles' busy footmarks, and was no longer the shabby rusty colour that suited the King so well.

'What you gone and done to it?' he roared. 'That ain't a palace, it is an ordinary white house.'

38

A Bottersnike called Glag went into raptures over the white clay. Glag would have liked to have been an artist. He painted when he could get the paint, using the tassel on his tail as a brush. This made his pictures big and bold and used up a great deal of paint, which was why he was usually short of it; but when he managed to finish a work of art it was worth looking at, especially from a distance of half a mile or more. Glag now found that the white clay, though it clogged the bristles of his tail, was ideal for splattering, and that if he threw it quick and hard enough it did not shrink his fingers.

'I will show you how a picture is made,' said Glag.

The King snorted. For him, pictures had to say something sensible or he was likely to sit on them. 'Stop daubing, Glag,' he ordered, 'and get and paint some signposts.'

The Bottersnikes blinked.

'Signposts!' the King shouted. 'Dozens of signposts. So's we don't get lost while we're looking for the nails.'

The King's idea was rather a good one. Around the lookout lay a jungle of prickly wattle, needlebush and sharp-leaved grasstrees, criss-crossed with pathways made by the wallabies, and in this thicket the Bottersnikes would soon get lost unless their way was marked by signposts.

'And the signposts will point us the way to the nails,' the Bottersnikes said happily. All of them were very hungry now.

'No they won't. A proper signpost should point the way home,' the King laid down.

Glag began painting pieces of wood and tin for signposts but his work was so artistic that the Bottersnikes could not tell from his pictures if they were coming or going. 'Sit on his head!' the King roared. 'We will use the Gumbles instead.'

'Gumbles ain't bright enough,' Chank was quick to say. 'We'd never see 'em in the dark.'

The King had an answer to this. He made the Gumbles get in the white house, where there was plenty of clay sticking to the walls, and had them rumbled and tumbled in there until they came out nicely whitened all over. Each Gumble was then twisted firmly around a short stick with one finger left straight to point the way.

'See?' said the King triumphantly. 'Signposts! We'll stick 'em in the ground all the way along. The little beggars can't escape while we're crashing about in the bush and they'll point the way home when we've found the nails.'

A top-notch idea! Better than Glag's fancywork. The Bottersnikes snuffled their noses loudly, which meant that they thought it funny, and gathered up their jam tins to put nails in. With their jam tins and their signposts they blundered into the jungle towards the setting sun, planting the signposts as they went. Chank took especial care to plant Tinkingumble first, pushing his stick firmly into the ground and hammering with a stone. 'This is the tinking one that causes all the bother,' Chank said. 'There! Tink your way out of that.'

For the Gumbles it was most uncomfortable, pointing one way all the time, and cold too as soon as the sun went down. The half moon was already high. Mournful little toots kept coming from Tootngumble. 'I can't help it,' he said. 'This is worse than being in a jam tin.'

They tried to make the best of it. Pretending they were telephone poles instead, they sent messages one to another along the line — gossipy stuff, to pass the time away. Presently an urgent telegram came from Jolligumble at the far end: BOTTERSNIKES HAVE FOUND NAILS STOP RETURNING SOON. Another flashed back from Tootngumble, who was next in line to Tink: TINKINGUMBLE HAD TINK STOP HOPE SOMETHING GOOD STOP.

Actually it sounded more of a ter-ink-le, perhaps because he was twisted like a corkscrew round his stick. 'That was an effort!' Tink said. 'I've just thought that if I could do a left turn I'd be pointing to the edge of the cliff and when they come back with the nails they'd all fall over.'

'That won't do us much good,' Tootngumble said.

'It won't do the Bottersnikes much good either. There is a forty-foot sheer drop. And it's not too close to Lyrebird's nest — I'm going to try it.' Tinkingumble wriggled and struggled to do a left turn on his stick but had to give up with a sigh. 'No good! I can't do it without help.'

And where was help going to come from? Tootngumble whispered: 'I don't think Tink's tinks are as good as they used to be.'

'They usually work,' Willigumble said stoutly.

Message! WALLABY IS HERE.

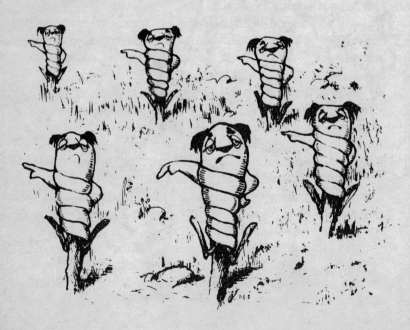

A pity it wasn't Possum, some of the Gumbles thought. Wallaby was a good-hearted creature as most grass-eaters are, but vague, and not at all clever with her front paws. She fumbled when she tried to untwist one or two of the signs and her claws were too sharp for comfort.

'Wallaby!' cried Tink. 'The very person! Give me a push with your hind foot, Wallaby, so that I do a left turn.'

Perplexed, Wallaby gave Tink a tap, not hard for fear of hurting him. Joey laughed at the strangeness of it. Grass and bushes tickled his face as he leaned from the pouch, watching.

'Not enough,' said Tink. 'Harder, please, Wallaby.'

'But I can't see why!' said the gentle clumsy creature.

'Because one good turn deserves another.' After the second push Tink's innocent finger pointed towards the forty-foot drop into darkness. 'And just in time, Wallaby, thanks!'

The King of the Bottersnikes appeared, leading his band. He was feeling huge. Their jam tins were brimful with delicious nails. The whitened Gumblesigns showed up beautifully in the moonlight, pointing the way home. 'Here we go left,' the King boomed jovially, 'here we go right. Here we go straight ahead.' He stopped when he saw Wallaby but was not afraid.

'Out of the way you rotten great kangaroo, shoo! Kangaroos are a pest and ought to be shot. Here we go left,' he said at the Tinkingumblesign, and waddled straight over the edge of the cliff.

For a second and a half there was complete silence, followed by a heavy *clunk!* as the King's head struck the rocks forty feet below. As so often happens when the King's head is sharply struck, a clever idea was driven into it, and for a moment the King sat in the dark at the bottom of the cliff all alone with his wonderful new idea.

CHAPTER FOUR

The King's Funeral

But not for long. The other Bottersnikes fell one by one after the King, clacking noisily on impact as their heads were not as sound as his. Mostly they knocked themselves cold on the rocks below and the King had to stamp and jump on them impatiently to bring them to their senses.

'This ain't no time to go to sleep! Wake up and listen, 'cos I've had the best idea what was ever thought of.'

'The King's had a clunk,' the Bottersnikes groaned. Most of them had horrible headaches.

When he had them sitting up and listening with red-hot ears the King announced: 'I am dead.'

The Bottersnikes opened their slanty eyes as wide as they would go.

'Killed by my fall. I have a broken neck, purple bruises and brain damage,' the King said. 'Death was instantaneous and total. I am a hundred percent deceased.'

'Long live the King!' said Chank feebly.

'And will have to be buried in a deep and comfortable grave with all the honours due to my exalted position,' the King went on, glaring at Chank. 'It will be a very grand occasion.'

Would there be a party, Snorg wanted to know.

'After!' the King shouted. 'First there will be a big procession with all the bands playing in black, and muffled cannon-fire, and this will let the Gumbles know something terrible has happened; being curious they'll be sure to come and see. When they come to pay their last respects I shall be lying in my open grave, looking passed-away and peaceful.'

'How dignified! How bewdiful!' the Bottersnikes agreed.

'Now then, the sound of all them Gumbles giggling round my grave will make me dangerously excited, and my whistle will blow, *freep-freep!*, like that, and that will be the signal for you lot to pounce out of hiding——'

'And shout "Got You!" '

'And grab 'em——'

'And pop 'em into jam tins! Hoo, hoo, hoo!'

'That's the best idea what ever came from a dead King!'

'Only thing,' Glob remarked, 'the Gumbles are caught already. They're twisted around sticks up top.'

'Idiot!' the King raged. 'Caught Gumbles are no good to us up top, what we want is to catch the Gumbles down here and that's what my funeral will do, so start digging my grave.' He prepared himself for a nap and ordered: 'Have my grave ready by the time I wake up.'

The Bottersnikes scratched at the soil with their fingers and scooped with their jam tins, having nothing else to dig with, and the hole they made might have been deep enough to bury a mouse if it was underprivileged and thin, or a butterfly, laid sideways. 'All very well for the King,' they growled, 'but for us as has got to do the diggin' it's murder.'

46

Chank would have nothing to do with it. 'It is Gumbles' work,' he said, and refused to get his hands dirtier. 'They are only giggling up there, doing nobody no good at all.'

As a matter of fact nearly all the giggles had gone out of those Gumblesigns by now. 'We shall be here for ever,' they were starting to think. 'Tinkingumble's sent all the Bottersnikes over the cliff, and who's going to pull us off these sticks now?' They were not angry about it, only a little sad that Tink's tinks seemed not quite as bright as they used to be.

'No, I didn't send them all over,' Tink said. 'I counted the clacks as they fell. One of them is still up here.'

Presently Glag came along the wallaby tracks, late because he was waddling backwards. The artist would sometimes waddle this way if he liked where he had come from better than where he was going. Sometimes, too, he would put his head between his legs to get a new view for his pictures, though his tail usually spoiled the effect.

Waddling backwards, Glag did not see the Tinkingumble-

sign and did not fall over the cliff. He stood where home used to be, wondering why everyone had gone out.

'Tink!' went Tinkingumble, more easily this time. 'Mr Glag, show us how you paint a picture,' he said artfully.

In all his life Glag the artist had never had the Gumbles entirely to himself. It would be a wonderful chance, he thought, to paint a glorious big picture on the rock using the white Gumbles as paint; he smirked a bit and told them: 'All right! I'll show you how it is done.'

So the Gumbles were pulled off their uncomfortable sticks at last, by Glag. It was so fine to be free they felt they could

leap over the dusty moon. Glag got them all together and stirred. He saw the big picture on the inside of his forehead; he would call it Moonscape Four. He put a bold streak of Gumblewhite across the grey rock. It looked fine. Then it began to wriggle. Glag stamped on it to make it keep still, with great care placed a white blob *there* and stood back to admire.

The blob ran away. Glag chased it and brought it back, by which time the streak had turned into a snake. Glag tried to straighten it but became tangled and lost control. His ears grew very red. To show his paint who was boss he jumped into it with both feet — what a splatter! Over the rock in all directions. 'That'll teach you to behave!' he shouted. Then, from the way the splash marks lay, he realised he had painted a picture.

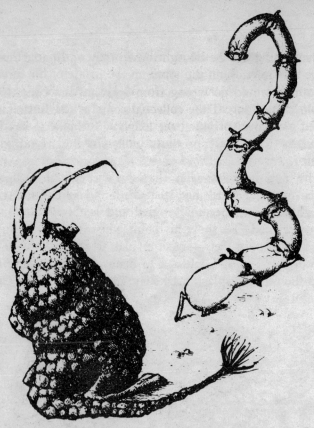

'I've done it!' yelled Glag, dancing. 'Moonscape Four!'

Only one person besides Glag saw that masterpiece — a sly watcher, a moonlight prowler: Fox. He came as silently as dewfall and startled both the artist and his paint. The Moonscape paint quivered, flowed into a big pool and began to pour itself over the cliff, away from where the Bottersnikes had fallen — a long drop, with no harm done as Gumbles' bones are not of the breakable kind. At the bottom they said 'Splash!' and giggled, squeezed each other to their proper shapes and became very serious. They climbed to the nest where, to their great relief, they found the mother lyrebird, brooding.

'Everything will be all right now,' they whispered reassuringly. 'We're back on the job.'

Nothing would go wrong from here on, the Gumbles determined, nothing. They collected some of the Bottersnikes' spilled nails and sprinkled the ledge with them, to vex Fox's feet if he tried that approach again. In the morning they would think of something better. Turn and turn about they stood sentry over the nest until daylight came. Chip-Chip was the best guarded chick in the whole bush that night. His mother was looking after him too.

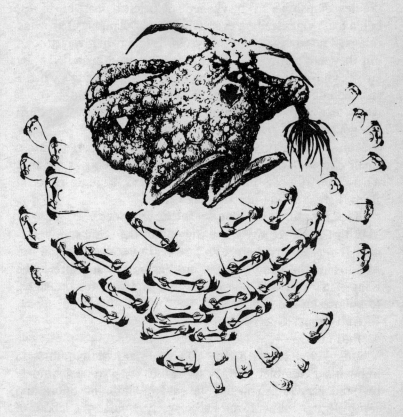

The Bottersnikes had no one to look after them and nothing to sleep under but their jam tins. Luckily there was no dew, or they would have shrunk to the size of matchboxes. When morning came they were ordinary sized and very grumpy, and the King, finding his grave scarcely deep enough to bury a big toe, rose to his full height and became very angry indeed.

'I want a grave, not a — *freep!* — mousehole!'

'There is nowhere to dig,' the Bottersnikes said sulkily. 'Look at it! The bush is just a mess.' At the foot of the cliff it was too rocky for anyone's grave. Farther down the slope the dense bush began: blackened sticks left by past bushfires, fallen logs, vines trailing everywhere and a clamour of growing things. The wombats and the lyrebirds knew their way around but they had pathways. The Bottersnikes were snatched at by lawyer vines, tripped by rotting logs, until the King's whistle shrilled like an angry referee. 'When we get the Gumbles back we'll clear all this, we'll chop it down and burn it. The bush has gone too far, *freep!* It has got to stop.'

More through fury than bushcraft the King barged into a small clearing with bare, loose earth — Lyrebird's mound, where the Gumbles had been earlier; and having a peaceful sleep there, snoring heartily, lay Chank.

'Kick him off,' the King said. 'Bury me here.'

With Chank removed, the digging of the King's grave began. It was easier where Lyrebird had scratched the soil up. About half the band was put to digging — 'and after,' the King said, 'you will hide in the fern and wait for the signal to pounce on the Gumbles.'

'And shout "Got You! ——" '

'And grab ——'

'Quiet!' the King roared. 'Do you want the Gumbles to know it's a Gumbletrap? My funeral is going to be genuinely real and very sad. You lot,' he said to Glob and Snorg and some of their cobbers who had cleverly avoided the labour of digging, 'start mourning.'

Glob and Co. blinked; they quite believed morning had started itself.

'Moaning and wailing to show the grief you feel,' the King shouted, bashing their heads with a log to give them a good start. 'And say some nice things about me, good and loud.'

The diggers scraped and scooped, the mourners moaned and wailed, the sun obligingly went behind a cloud to cast a grey gloom over the graveside scene. The King sat majestically tickling his tummy with the end of his tail while his grave deepened inch by inch. He felt highly pleased with himself and his solemn funeral, until the mope and mourn of it was spoiled by long, loud, rattling, raspberry-flavoured snores.

The King's whistle shrilled instantly. 'Snoring ain't proper! My funeral's a sad and solemn thing, especially for me, and no one ain't snoring while I'm being buried.'

All the Bottersnikes were by chance awake. After their heads had been well bashed for snoring it was observed that the snorer was only a bird — 'a rotten old feather duster with a long tail, and the fool thing isn't even asleep.'

'Wring its neck. Sit on its head,' the King ordered.

Lyrebird ran off to another of his mounds. He had been trying out this new sound, learned from Chank, to see if it would fit into one of his concerts.

Soon the grave was deep enough to do. The King decided they would have to manage without the bandmarch and the cannonfire as these things would take too long to arrange. Instead, Chank wrote a bold notice in charcoal on the bark of a blue gum:

5c TO SEE THE DED KING

'But of course we will let the Gumbles in free,' Chank smirked.

Now the solemn time had come for the King's interment. He stood on the pile of earth at the end of his grave, glaring. In case he should go to sleep in his grave before the Gumbles came, it would be a good idea to have a vine tied to his foot which someone could pull as a signal. So the King said: 'Tie a string to my toe. At the proper time, pull it.'

With these last words, the King very majestically fell backwards into his grave, and lay.

While the grave was being dug Glob and Snorg and the rest had done their job as mourners extra well, making such moans as trees might make, if they had voices, while being eaten by termites, or while having their branches wrenched in a wild storm.

'Hark at that!' the Gumbles said. 'Are they having a party, d'you think?'

'We must know what is going on for Chip-Chip's sake as well as our own,' said Happigumble. 'We had better find out.'

'I'll go and spy,' said Willi.

'No, you'll get caught, better if we all go. Everyone be careful.'

'We always are!'

'What if it's a trap?' said Jolligumble.

'It'll be all right if we are careful. We only get caught when we're not expecting it.'

'I'll probably have a toot if anything's wrong.'

So they decided to go and see. Glob and Co. were rolling on the ground, kicking up their heels for grief. 'Have you got tummy aches?' the Gumbles asked, 'or blisters on the feet?'

For some nice things to say about their King the mourners had tried 'the good King is dead' and 'the King is dead, good!' and had decided it would be best to say 'the King is good and dead!', and they told the Gumbles this, with sobs of sorrow.

'Killed by his fall,' howled Glob. 'He has a broken brain, damaged bruises and a purple neck.'

'And you must go and pay your last respects,' Snorg wailed, 'while he is looking peaceful and passed-out.'

'It's a trap,' Jolligumble muttered.

'No no, no more Gumbletraps, never no more ——'

'No more shoutin' "Got You" and grabbin', and bungin' you in jam tins,' said Glob. 'Can't you see? We are too over-come with grief.'

'Ain't we making it plain?' Snorg said rather angrily. 'We are paralysed with sorrow, we couldn't grab a saucepan handle.'

'Don't go near,' warned Merrigumble. 'You can never trust a Bottersnike.'

'Not Bottersnikes!' Glob shouted. 'From here on we're going to be Bettersnikes.'

'Except the King — he's dead and gone, he's good and dead,' they moaned together. 'Oh woe, woe, woe!'

Once roused, Gumbles' curiosity itches and itches until it is satisfied. Very cautiously they went on, using one of Lyre-bird's tunnels in the fern. They saw Chank's notice and stud-ied it for clues. Then they saw the earth thrown up. 'What a lot of digging! This is not like Bottersnikes at all,' they thought.

The King was lying very still. The digging party had hidden themselves completely. There was no snoring. Now the Gum-bles could see the tips of the King's ears sticking out of the grave.

'They really have buried him!' they whispered in awe.

'And it was me that made him fall,' said Tink, with round eyes.

They tiptoed onwards. Into the presence of the dead King. Someone pulled the vine that had been tied to the King's toe, to warn him. The Gumbles did not notice this. The Gumbles saw nothing move. They were nearly in the danger zone, not quite, when the whistle shrilled. Tootngumble's warning toot couldn't be heard in the row. *Freep freep free-ep!* Piercing, unmistakable.

Out crashed the grabbers, as though they had been trained. Pounding and pouncing all over the graveside. They caught nothing — there was nothing to catch.

'Bunglers! Idiots!' the dead King raged. 'You pounced too soon!'

'You blew the whistle!' they yelled.

The King rose from his grave to an awful height. 'I didn't blow the whistle!'

'Well somebody blew a whistle — there it goes again!' and again and again, but not from the King's stomach only. Gradually the truth soaked in, between their scorching ears: 'That bird! That rotten bird with a long tail ——'

'Lyrebird!' the Gumbles cried, as they scuttled to safety. 'Lyrebird copied the whistle and sprang the trap too soon!'

* * *

CHAPTER FIVE

The Art of Catching Gumbles

Tinks happen at the strangest times. A real beauty came to
Tinkingumble as they were running for their lives from the
King's grave — *tink!*, sweet and fruity as a home-made cake.

'I've thought of a way to make Chip-Chip safer.'

'Got to make ourselves safer first,' Happigumble puffed.

'A catapult!' Tink said. 'To shoot anyone who tries to go
along the ledge.'

It seemed a wonderful idea. Making the catapult was easy
for the Gumbles, who love playing with springy things, levers,
see-saws and suchlike. They chose two swishy saplings on the
edge of the dense bush not far from the nest and tied their
tops together with vines, binding in a piece of stringybark to

hold the bullets. They used a longer vine-rope to pull the saplings back, and when released the bullets shot out with plenty of sting. After practice they could fire oak knobs and cabbage-palm seeds in salvoes and pepper the target usually.

'That'll warm Fox up a bit,' they chuckled.

To make Chip-Chip safer still, Happigumble suggested they should climb the cliff and collect some stones to drop. 'Then if anyone tries to raid the nest we can pepper him from the side and bomb him from the top as well.'

That would be splendid. Everyone agreed. 'Gumblerope, then, and up the cliff,' Happigumble said. Then came a second tink, clear as a magpie on a frosty morning. 'Quicker if I fire you up the catapult! I'll alter the aim.'

Willigumble wanted first go but they told him it was too dangerous. Glag was still up there. 'Fire us up one after the other as quick as you can,' Happigumble said. 'We'll soon take care of Glag. Willi, you can help Tink with the firing.'

'The Bottersnikes are coming!' said Jolligumble.

They worked like horses, Tink and Willi, firing the others up. The catapult had masses of power. It sent the Gumble-bullets whistling skywards till they disappeared over the edge of the cliff. 'Won't old Glag get the surprise of his life?' Willi giggled. 'How I'd like to see his face when they all come dropping in.' Tink and Willi chuckled at the good job they had done. They thought they had done a really good job.

* * *

Glag the artist had wonderful pictures in his head, waiting to be painted. He had yards of flat rock to paint on, and no one to waddle in his work while it was wet or to sit on his head while it was seeing pictures; but he had no paint.

He tried to make some by stirring soil into a pool of water but the sloppy mixture caused his tail to shrink. Charcoal did not suit his style — it crumbled under his bold strokes — and the clay had gone hard. Glag began to get desperate when a

truly bright idea dropped into his head. The Bottersnikes'
custom, when they wanted a home, was to crawl under any
old bit of rubbish they could find — sheets of iron, tins,
baths, tanks, anything would do if it kept the rain off. It
seemed to Glag that this was not a dainty habit. With a little
care, a little flair, Bottersnikes' homes could be made attractive. So it came to him in a flash what he would do: he would
design a beautiful rubbish heap and live in it.

Glag collected all the building materials he could find. His
prize piece was an iron bedstead with knobs and rails. He
stood this on end and hung a watering can on one of the legs.
The springs of the bed were ideal for holding bits of rag or
paper; he stuck them in the wires and they would stay there
and flutter. Glag worked in a fire of enthusiasm. 'A blob!' he
said — Glag was a great user of blobs — 'I need a blob, I
need a blob, I need a blob.'

With a twang in the bedsprings a blob appeared — the very
thing he needed, squashy and squeezable to any shape. He
was too wrapped up in his work to wonder how it got there.
Several more followed in quick succession, out of the sky it
seemed, and Glag had to work like mad arranging them in
their proper places. When he stood back to admire his work
he felt it was coming along very nicely; and the catapulted

Gumbles, who found themselves twisted and looped into the springs of the bed, wondered how in the name of science or politics they came to be caught in a Gumbletrap like this.

'You know,' said Happigumble sadly, 'I really do think Tink's tinks are not as bright as they used to be.'

Perhaps it was not fair to put all the blame on Tink. He and Willi knew nothing of what had happened and had no time to wonder about it; as they catapulted the last of their mates up the Bottersnikes came waddling along from the direction of the King's grave.

'Now you, Willi. Quick.'

'No, I'll stay with you.'

'We'll have to run for it then. Come on.'

Tink and Willi ran a little way down the slope to be out of the Bottersnikes' path. They found the father Lyrebird down there, scratching the earth for insects.

'Lyrebird!' said Willi. 'There are Bottersnikes everywhere.

60

Don't you think you could look after Chip-Chip now and then? It would make things easier for everyone.'

'Who is Chip-Chip?'

'Your chick! He's the one who'll sing and dance when you're — well, when you're too old to sing and dance. Someone's got to carry on,' Willigumble said. 'So couldn't you help?'

Lyrebird went on scratching. 'I wouldn't mind,' he said. 'But it's the wife. She won't have me near the nest.'

Tink and Willi looked at each other and sighed.

'She says she goes to a lot of trouble to hide it and she won't have me showing everyone where it is. I haven't even seen the chick.' For a moment Lyrebird looked as if he were going to moult. 'But I don't care! What do I want with nests? I dance! I sing!' He threw his head back and carolled at his loudest, blending in bird calls, Chank's snores and the King's whistles.

'Not so loud!' said Tink anxiously. 'The Bottersnikes will hear.'

They had. Furious shouts from higher up told that this time Lyrebird had sung too heartily. 'There he is!' the King

was heard to thunder. 'That rotten bird that spoiled my Gumbletrap! *Get him!*'

The mourners and the gravediggers, led by the lately dead King himself, came down the hill like robbers running, like words tumbling from a dictionary, to have their revenge on Lyrebird. Going downhill they could move amazingly fast. Some of them lay on their sides and rolled, which was quicker still.

Lyrebird ran across the slope, keeping low, and watched the Bottersnikes roll past. No one was likely to catch him in his own fernbed. Tink and Willi scooted down the hill, bumping and sliding, until the land flattened out. They pushed through thick wiry grass and found themselves on the edge of a creek where the water trickled over shallows into deep pools, almost hidden by the crowding grasses on the banks.

'Got a tink?' asked Willi, panting.

'Don't think so. Wait . . . Yes!'

Willi had the same idea at the same moment. Giggling, they splashed through the water where it was shallow and hid under a tree root on the far bank. Most of the Bottersnikes had rolled to a standstill. Small fires burned in their ears from pieces of dry bracken picked up during the roll.

'Which way'd he go? Don't let him get away!' the King roared.

Tinkingumble sang out: 'Quick, Lyrebird! Don't let them catch you!'

'*Freep-freep!*' went Willi. His squeaky voice copied the whistle as cleverly as Lyrebird would have done.

'We've got him cornered!' the King yelled triumphantly. 'He's in that long grass. I'll throw a party for the one what catches him.'

The Bottersnikes charged into the grass, grabbing-mad. 'Got you!' they started to shout, out of habit. None of them saw the deep, still rock pool until too late. Their charge carried them right into the icy shock of the water. Steam hissed up in clouds from their red-hot ears. But very soon their splashes became smaller and their yells became little bleats as the water shrank, and shrank, and shrank them . . . their fat stomachs, their warts and knobbles, their absurd ears . . . until they were no more than matchbox models of themselves with only their bad tempers life-sized.

When they were about the size of brown frogs Tink and

Willi fished them out with long sticks and set them spluttering on the bank. The King was speechless. While every other part of him had shrunk his swallowed whistle had not. Now the tiny King was so full of whistle he could not pass a single comment, but sat like a toad, bulging.

'We could teach him to hop,' Willi giggled.

Tinkingumble thought it would be better to send them home at once, while they were still small enough to manage. For they would grow, slowly, as the wind dried them. Willi, king-sized among all those shrunk 'snikes, gave the orders: he lined them up with a stick and drove them uphill to the catapult. Taking great care not to get scorched on the red-hot needles of their ears, Tink and Willi fired them up in threes

and fours to the top of the cliff — sent them flying home. 'And now the lyrebirds can have some peace,' Tink said.

'We've done a good job, just the two of us,' said Willi. 'The others ought to be jolly pleased.'

'I'll fire you up and you can tell them what we've done.'

'No, you go, they might need your tinks up there.'

It seemed strange that there were no pleased shouts from the top when the tiny 'snikes came flying home, and no sign either of the bombs that Happigumble's party was supposed to collect. Tink agreed to go up and see what had been happening. Willi pulled on the catapult with his whole weight,

which was just enough to give Tink the necessary boost. 'Here I am!' Tink yelled as he sailed over the edge of the cliff. 'What's everybody doing — O grasshop ——!'

Tink struck Glag's house as the rest had done, but lower down; Glag made him into a letterbox for his front door and felt that his house was perfect.

The tiny Bottersnikes had been no use at all to Glag for building. Hard pellety things, they rattled off the house like hailstones. Wrinkling his nose, Glag pushed them into a heap with his foot and swept them under the carpet.

Tink was miserable when he saw what his catapult had done. 'I thought it was such a good idea,' he said.

'It's not as bad as being in a jam tin,' said Happigumble, who had been made into a hanging flowerpot. 'And we don't have to worry too much about Chip-Chip. Fox has gone away. We heard some crows talking about him. He's heading for a farm where they keep poultry.'

Tink brightened a little.

'And the Bottersnikes are too small to do any harm — except Glag, and he thinks of nothing but his house.'

'And Willi's down there,' Tink whispered. 'He might be able to think of a way to help.'

Willi was already doing this. By now he had realised something was very wrong at the top. 'They must be in a jam up there; they'll need me to get them out of it,' he said thoughtfully. 'I'd better go and spy.' Willigumble left the catapult and made his way towards the cliff, and there received quite a nasty shock. A Bottersnike, a full-sized Bottersnike, was lying in the fern asleep.

'Smiggles!' gasped Willi.

Everyone had forgotten Smiggles. This was easy to do as a dreamer is a person of no importance when he is not dreaming. Smiggles had been lying at the bottom of the cliff ever since the rescue of the palace-mobile, unconscious at first, now sleeping peacefully.

And it was not safe to leave him there — so close to the lyrebird's nest. Willi pondered the problem anxiously. 'Suppose he dreams a gun? I think I'd better throw stones at him till he wakes and — O grasshoppers!' Willi cried, looking closer at the knobbly form in the fern, 'it's too late! He *is* dreaming!'

CHAPTER SIX

The Artist and the Dreamer

The trouble with Smiggles was that his dreams became not true exactly, but solid, so that everyone could see what had been going on in his sleeping mind. Sometimes the things he dreamed were useful, just as often they were not; either way it made him different from the others and they seldom let him forget it.

Whilst lying in the fern Smiggles dreamed that he was climbing easily up the cliff by ladder. Far below him the others shouted: 'Help us, Smiggles! Tell us what to do!' Smiggles waved to them and climbed on. Yet no matter how far he climbed he never reached the top.

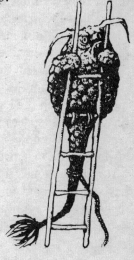

When he woke he saw that his dream ladder was still leaning against the cliff, firm and strong, no rungs missing, though too short by a few feet to reach the top. Smiggles was extremely annoyed with the cliff for being too big for his beautiful dream. With a few pounds of dynamite he could have made the cliff low enough to fit. Having none, he did the next best thing: he climbed to the topmost rung but one and yelled for help.

Glag heard him and looked over the edge. He was not at all pleased to see the dreamer on his ladder. Glag enjoyed being the only full-sized Bottersnike, with a fine house to live in and all the Gumbles to himself; it was a very good arrangement. Between the legs of his bed he had raised a wall of kero tins, with big spaces for windows and blinds to keep out the view. The Gumbles were looped and twisted wherever a bit of decoration was needed. The only thing that worried Glag was that his house so far lacked a roof. If it rained he would have to move out and live in a bucket. What he needed to make his house quite perfect was a sound, weatherproof roof — that, and a large supply of food for his larder. Given these he saw no reason why he should not live the rest of his life in ease and elegance. Looking down at Smiggles a wonderful idea came to him for obtaining both.

'Pull me up!' yelled Smiggles.

'All right,' said Glag. 'Hey Smig, have a look in that nest before you come up.'

'Not likely! There is a horrid monster in there.'

'Then I won't pull you up.'

'Glag, come back!' Smiggles wailed. 'What do you want the monster for?'

Glag snuffled. The idea he had in his head was good enough to make the world spin faster. 'We'll make a deal with Fox. We'll catch the monster and put it in a cage, Smig, till we see Fox; then we'll give him the monster to eat if he tells us where to find a mattress. I shall put the mattress on top of my house and it will be a wonderful roof to keep the rain out.'

'Don't be silly,' Smiggles said. 'Mattresses are for eating.'

'We'll eat the corners when we're hungry — it'll last us for weeks. It's only you and me, Smig, all the rest are small. And you can dream some paint and I'll paint lots of pictures.'

Smiggles thought about this. He very badly wanted to go up in the world and Glag was the only one who could help him. Once he was up there Smiggles reckoned he would soon find a chance to push the artist over the cliff, or perhaps brain him with his own easel.

'Just you and me, Glag?'

'And a mattress all to ourselves. And the Gumbles to look after us. And you can dream all day and I'll paint pictures.'

'All right then,' said Smiggles hoarsely. 'I'll do it. I'll catch the monster.' He climbed slowly down the ladder trembling at the thought of what he had to do. It would not be so bad if he did not have to look at it. Smiggles closed his eyes, held his breath and put his hand carefully into the nest opening. The monster did not peck or bite. It felt quite soft and helpless. 'Got you!' Smiggles faltered. But he did not dare to look at it.

At the top of the cliff Glag's house rattled as the Gumbles strained to free themselves. But there was nothing they could do. Glag had fastened them with care; they were prisoners as

surely as if they had been squashed into jam tins. Glag took no notice of the rattling, of their protests. He had tied an empty paint tin to the King's fishing line and now lowered this to Smiggles.

'Hurry up, Smig. Put the monster in the paint pot.'

'Haul me up first,' growled Smiggles, who was not going to be left behind by a trick.

With a heave and a grunt, up came the dreamer. Together they hauled up the paint tin and its precious contents.

'That ain't much of a monster, Smig! Put it between two bits of bread and you wouldn't have a sandwich.'

Smiggles was enormously proud of himself now he had done the deed, and of his monster. 'Not big, but savage! You should hear the noise it makes. Like that!'

'Chip-chip!' very piercing, came from the tin.

The Gumbles' sighs whispered like a sad wind all round the house. 'Gumbles on guard we were supposed to be,' they said miserably, 'and here we are stuck on a pile of rubbish while Chip-Chip ends up in a paint pot.'

'Willi's still free,' Tinkingumble remembered. 'Perhaps he'll think of something.'

'But he's so little, what can he do?'

'He might — think of something,' said Tink. Trying to be cheerful.

Glag was waiting for Smiggles to say something nice about his house. Smiggles said: 'That is a rum sort of house. I thought it was a disaster in a coalmine.'

'It's more than a house, it's a work of art — it's a sculpture,' Glag told him haughtily. 'As it happens to be hollow you can live in it real comfortable. All it needs is a tasty roof, which we shall get when we see Fox.' He patted the tin and smirked.

'My monster's not safe in there, he might jump out the top. He ought to be in a proper cage.'

'A cage!' Glag was pleased with the idea. 'It would look

73

good in front of my house. And we can fatten the monster up.'

They began at once, raking through the rubbish Glag had not used for his house. Nothing resembling a cage was to be found. Glag and Smiggles tramped the scrub with red ears. They pulled out stuff that had lain for years rusting and rotting quietly, and such disturbance did they make that two passing crows paused in their flight to see if anything interesting was being turned up. They perched in a nearby tree and cleared their throats.

'There has been sport,' said one. 'Fox raided the poultry farm and took more than he needed.'

'Then there will be meat on the bones he leaves!'

'We shall soon see — he is coming back. With a fat hen in his mouth, he is heading this way.' The two crows cawed and gurgled.

'Grasshoppers! Did you hear that?' cried Happigumble. 'We've got to get Chip-Chip out of that tin, and quickly. Can't someone think of something?' Unfortunately, the Gumbles were as helpless as before. Being squashy — useful at times — means that when stuck you are stuck absolutely until deliverance comes.

'Any chance of a tink?'

'I'm trying,' the letterbox replied. 'It's hard to be bright when you're hollow inside.'

'If only Willi would show up! He could help.'

Having failed to find a cage, Glag and Smiggles decided to build one. They took a lot of care and fashioned a strong, cumbersome rattletrap of a cage from pieces of tin and wire. They forgot to build a door to it and had to press the wires apart to slip the monster in. To ensure the cage itself did not escape, or roll over the cliff, they tied it to the house with the plastic rope, part of which was still fastened to Smiggles' tail. The monster was most secure. They covered the cage with a bag and snuffled.

'He won't get out of that!'

'Not till he goes into Fox.'

'Hurry up, Fox!' they yelled into the bush.

The Gumbles put on a bit of a bluster and tried to tell them that Fox wouldn't be coming as he was taking up poultry for a living, but it did no good. 'Them Gumbles ought to be in jam tins,' Smiggles said, and started to pull them off.

'Leave 'em alone!' Glag screeched, sticking them on as fast as Smiggles pulled them off. 'They are my decorations. Smiggles! *Smiggles!* This is my house and they're my decorations.'

'They're half mine,' Smig retorted. 'I'll have my half in jam tins.'

Bit by bit the partnership of the artist and the dreamer turned to a furious shouting match, then to a full-scale battle with feet and fists and red-hot ears. The Gumbles watched hopefully. Some good should come from such a fierce battle, they felt. One of the fighters might cannon into the house, knock it down and shake some Gumbles free. Before this happened there was a sudden toot from Tootngumble and the others froze. Fox appeared, picking his way between the rocks above the lookout. He paused to watch the fight, one paw raised. Smiggles was grinding his heel into Glag's tail; Glag had Smiggles in a headlock and was punching his face with his free hand, until he too saw Fox.

'Fox!' Glag shouted, landing a last vicious punch. 'Me and him is business partners. We got a deal to discuss with you.'

'I mind my own business,' said Fox. He continued his dainty-footed walk to the edge of the cliff and glanced down to the nest.

'It's no good looking down there,' Glag told him. 'We've captured the monster——'

'*I* captured the monster. You can have him to eat, Fox——'

'If you show us where to find a mattress.'

'I'm not hungry,' Fox said. 'I have eaten fowl.'

'But you'll be hungry tomorrow——'

'Or in ten minutes' time,' Smiggles added. 'And the monster is in a cage, fattening, so you can keep him as long as you like.'

Fox seemed interested. 'Really? Show me.'

'You show us the mattress first,' they said, businesslike.

Fox was a craftier schemer than Glag or Smiggles. He decided to get the two 'snikes well out of the way while he took a look around; pretending to search his memory he said:

'Let's see, the best mattress I know is round the back of ——. No, that's not the best; people like you will want nothing but the best, and that you will find a little way down the road, under a tree with branches.'

'We'll find it!' They nudged each other and snuffled as they went off to look. 'He knows more than one! We'll find fault with the first and make him show us the second before we give him the monster.'

Alone now at the lookout, Fox stared again towards the nest, then at Glag's extraordinary house. Was it a trap? He padded warily around it, keeping a safe distance. He paused under the cage. His nose seemed to quiver.

Silently, the Gumbles screamed: 'Don't move, Chip-Chip! Don't make a sound!'

Fox reached upwards and with a front paw touched the cage gingerly, making it swing. There was a little rustling noise inside, and a feather floated to the ground.

CHAPTER SEVEN

Dump Development Scheme

Fox sat back on his haunches and eyed the cage greedily. With one spring, he reckoned, he could strike the cage from its hook. He coiled himself.

'Something's burning!' cried Jolligumble suddenly.

'The house!' Merrigumble shouted. 'It's on fire!'

It was no hoax, either, to put Fox off: smoke was rising, choking grey smoke, from somewhere inside. Fox backed away and sat down at a distance. He wasn't hungry enough to risk getting burned for a mouthful of dinner. But the Gumble-decorations were helpless, pinned on the burning house, as was Chip-Chip in his cage.

Luckily it was not a serious blaze. An old bag, which was Glag's carpet, had started smouldering from the heat of the Bottersnikes' ears as they lay beneath it, where Glag had swept them. They crawled out, tiny, damp and shivery, blew on the bag to make it glow and fed it with paper and small sticks until they had a warming blaze. As Glag had not built a chimney smoke poured from the door and windows, making the fire look worse than it really was.

Usually when shrunk Bottersnikes must wait for the wind to dry them before returning to normal size, which may take half a day or longer. With a nice fire going they dried out rapidly and grew about two inches a minute, all their warts and knobbles coming back, their grating voices, the toadstools on their eyebrows; and a certain idea that was in the King's head swelled and swelled as the space in his skull increased.

That lyrebird, the King had been thinking. Who was it that spoiled the well-planned Gumbletrap? Who caused the Bottersnikes to fall in the creek? Who snored at the King's funeral?

Lyrebird.

'That bird must be got rid of,' the King squeaked. He was about the size of a rat with a voice to match. 'All lyrebirds must be got rid of so's it never happens again.'

'Down with them long-tailed birds!' the Bottersnikes chorused.

'And them with short tails,' the King said, growing an inch, 'and them with curved beaks and gaudy feathers! What's the good of birds? They only flit around and wake you at dawn with their twitterin'.'

Birds made dawn hideous with their twittering, the growing 'snikes agreed.

'Do away with 'em! Animals too,' the King said, being then as big as a bandicoot. 'Snakes! Lizards! What good do they do? They only take up room and breathe the air.'

'Taking up our space!' screeched the Bottersnikes, who now filled the floor of Glag's house around the fire and, still growing, had nowhere to go but upward. 'Breathing our air! We are the only things that matter — naturally.'

Pressed upwards in the throng, the King put one foot on Glob's head, the other on Chank's shoulder, and was tall enough to look out of the window. 'All that land,' he said, shaking his fist at the view, 'is only fit for kangaroos and crows.'

'And who wants to be a kangaroo?' the Bottersnikes said indignantly. 'Or a crow?'

'We'll clear it. We'll chop it down and burn it. We'll make it nice and level so's we can waddle where we like, and sleep where we like. And there won't be no animals making a nuisance nor no birds to wake us.'

'They'll all be dead,' the Bottersnikes shouted. 'Hoo, hoo, hoo!'

'Instead of all them trees we'll fill it up with rubbish,' the King went on, he and his idea nearly full-sized now. 'Avenues and avenues of rubbish! Beautifully arranged into palaces for elegant livin'! Fountains that don't work! Sculptures ——'

'We'll feel at home wherever we go!' the Bottersnikes crowed delightedly. 'Livin' will be pure pleasure!'

So great was the crush in Glag's house, the surging excitement as they grew, that the King was squeezed from the window and fell heavily. 'This place is too small,' he stormed, kicking it. 'We want room to expand. We want space. What we want,' the King said, full-sized at last, 'is a Dump Development Scheme. To make a World Fit for Bottersnikes.'

This put the Bottersnikes in a frenzy. They came pouring from Glag's house into the open, then paused, blinking angrily

at the unimproved world they saw and ready to kick things. 'We want Development!' they chanted. 'We want a Better World!' Finding the Gumbles hanging about the house doing nothing the Bottersnikes pulled them off and shouted: 'You heard what we want! Well, get busy on some development.'

The Gumbles were delighted to be released, though there was no chance of escape with the Bottersnikes so worked up — besides, Chip-Chip had to be rescued somehow and returned to his nest. With the Bottersnikes in their present mood Chip-Chip was in dreadful danger. Glag's house was being bashed and kicked because it was so far from perfect, and after a loud protest from Glob and Snorg the covered cage slipped from its hook and fell. Toot and Jolligumble ran to it, dragged it inside the house to save it being trampled. 'Chip-Chip, are you all right?'

'Well, it was a bit of a bump,' said a familiar voice, a squeaky one. 'They might have warned me.'

'Willigumble! — is that you?' they cried, astonished. 'How did you get in there — and what have you done to yourself?' For Willi had done his best to change himself into a bird. He had squeezed his nose into a sort of beak, stuck feathers round

his middle and made flappers from his arms, something like a penguin's. 'I always wanted to be a lyrebird, didn't I?' Willi said a trifle sadly. 'I can't dance well enough to be a proper one but as a chick I'm good enough to fool Glag and Smiggles.'

'Where's the real Chip-Chip?'

'In his nest, of course. When I heard Glag and Smiggles plotting I knew I had to do something so I pushed Chip-Chip to the back of the nest and covered him with feathers and when Smiggles put his hand in he grabbed me. He had his eyes shut anyway.'

'Willi, you can't stay there, it's too dangerous.'

'I must! As long as Fox thinks I'm Chip-Chip he won't raid the nest again,' Willi pointed out. He was right, of course. Fox had slunk away when the Bottersnikes became big and noisy but he would be back, nothing surer, as soon as he felt hungry.

'Hang on for a bit then, Willi. We'll get you out as soon as it's safe.' Toot and Jolligumble covered the cage carefully.

The Bottersnikes were becoming impatient for some progress towards a better world. 'We can't wait all day,' they said, stamping, and the King announced: 'I shall be ready for the grand opening of my Dump Development Scheme in five minutes.'

'We can't do everything at once!' the Gumbles protested.

'Yes you can! All you got to do is think faster.'

The Gumbles went into a huddle to decide what was to be done. Some of them felt a bit gloomy. If the Bottersnikes didn't get what they wanted they would become crankier and crankier and nothing would be safe. Happigumble considered the best thing to do with difficult 'snikes was to give them a good feed and take their minds off other things. 'I know, we'll give them a banquet,' he said.

'But think of all the work!'

'Glag and Smiggles are doing the hardest part for us,' Happigumble remarked. 'When they come back with a mattress we'll stick it on the roof and barbecue it and there's their banquet. We'll have to build a big fire inside.'

It seemed a good solution, one that might stop the Bottersnikes damaging the scenery beyond repair. The Gumbles went to work, making Glag's house large enough to be a banqueting hall, and strengthening the walls with logs, stones, anything they could find, to carry the weight of the mattress-roof. They had to hurry. They could tell from shouts and groans and the cracking of small trees that Glag and Smiggles were on the way home with something big and troublesome. When the two 'snikes appeared they were carrying a double mattress on their heads. Their red-hot ears had burned small holes in it already.

Glag and Smiggles were horrified to see what had happened while they were away: the Bottersnikes grown big, the King

bawling and bossy again, Glag's house altered out of all recognisable shape. The mattress they had struggled to bring home was taken from them and hoisted to the housetop, where it made a splendid roof. The house really looked something now, like the abode of a wild man in the woods. As they gathered wood for the barbecue fire the Gumbles felt it was almost a pity it had to be burned.

But burned it was. The Gumbles filled it with dry branches, twigs, leaves and bracken, then got a light from Chank's ears — Chank was red-hot because he would have liked to have invented the barbecue himself. The dry kindling flared, shooting tongues of flame to the roof, which quickly began to char and smoulder. The Bottersnikes hooed and hooted in the smoke. They saw now how it was going to work. When the mattress was cooked the Gumbles would rake the fire out so that the Bottersnikes could go in to the banquet. They could sleep off the effects of over-eating in the ashes, which would be nice and warm to lie in, and afterwards they would be left with an interesting piece of sculpture as part of the King's Development Scheme. So it was really a centrally-heated sculptural barbecue-banqueting hall, and the King was quite pleased with the progress.

'I shall open it as the first building in my Dump Development,' he announced. 'After the banquet.'

The Bottersnikes had never held a banquet before though they frequently threw parties. These would go on for three days or longer getting rowdier and rowdier until there was nothing left to throw. The Gumbles hated them. A banquet, they hoped, would be more dignified. They were quite wrong.

The Bottersnikes couldn't wait to begin. Before the banqueting hall was properly cool enough to enter they hopped in and tried to stamp out the embers with their horny feet. By jumping from the hot floor they could snatch handfuls of

smouldering stuffing from the roof, but this was inconvenient
and tended to give them the hiccups. They overcame this by
sending half the Gumbles aloft with forked sticks. The Bottersnikes stood beneath with their mouths open and caught
the hot stuffing as the Gumbles forked it down. A great
success. 'Now my Dump Development Scheme is working
we'll have banquets every day,' the King said.

It was hot and dangerous work for the Gumble-forkers.
The whole house rocked as the Bottersnikes pushed and
shoved for their share of the banquet. It may have been this
that gave Tink what he afterwards described as the brightest
tink he'd ever had — luckily the Bottersnikes did not hear it
over the chomping noises from their own teeth.

'If we could only make the house fall down!' Tink said.

The other forkers thought Tink was off his rocker again.

'Don't you see? They're all standing in their stuffing themselves. If the place was to crash on top of them their banqueting hall would become ——'

'A prison!' squeaked Tootngumble.

It would too. The bed would fall legs uppermost, pinning the Bottersnikes beneath, while the logs and stones used in the building would crash along the sides to stop them crawling from beneath.

'We'd catch them all in one go and keep them there till Chip-Chip is grown up, then we'd only have Fox to worry about.'

Tootngumble climbed down the house to tell the others of this wonderful idea. Could it be made to work? Pulling the house down with a rope would be best, they decided; the plastic rope was still tied to Willi's cage, which had been moved before the barbecue fire was lit. Happigumble threw up the free end of it to Tink, who tied it to the top of the iron bedstead. Only half the Gumbles could do the pulling, the others had to fork like mad to keep the Bottersnikes busy. They strained and tugged on the rope. The house rocked a little, nothing more. It was strongly built. After a second try the pullers realised Tink's bright idea made too big a task for them.

'We can't do it without help,' Happigumble said glumly.

Unexpectedly help came, though it did not seem so at first to the worried Gumbles. On the rocks above them there appeared — of all sights they least wished to see! — the sly form of Fox.

'That's all we need!' the Gumbles groaned. 'We can't deal with Fox and the Bottersnikes at the same time.'

Fox sat on the rocks and looked down curiously at the Banquetsnikes. They had eaten three-quarters of the mattress now and the King, who by standing on the others' shoulders had had his full share, decided to call a break. For when having a party the Bottersnikes liked to stuff themselves as full as they could possibly get, have a brief rest, then go on again. As his stomach was too full for the whistle to blow the

King waved his arms and shouted 'Half time!', then, glaring round for anyone who might care to argue, his eye fell by chance on Fox.

'Ha, Fox!' he boomed. 'Come and have —— ' He nearly said *a feed* but changed his mind at the last moment. '—— a look at my central eating barbecued sculpture-hall banquet. I just designed it and built it and now I'm going to open it as the first building in my Dump Development Scheme.'

'I have come,' Fox said, 'for what is in that cage.'

And then the Gumbles realised they had left the rescue of Willi perilously late. Toot and Merrigumble ran to the cage but the King was there before them, to make sure that what Fox wanted was nothing he wanted himself. Glag and Smiggles rushed out too, alarmed for their monster. The King laid hold of the cage and shook it violently.

'Chip *chip!*' cried Willi.

'There is something in there,' the King said intelligently, and ripped off the bag cover. There was Willi sitting in a small pool of feathers. Willi looked most odd — partly bird-shaped still, partly frightened Gumble, and the King did not know what to make of him at all. 'What do you want that for, Fox?'

Fox came slowly to the cage and sniffed the feathers, which were genuine lyrebird. Willi shivered.

'Hey! You can't give the monster away! He's ours,' Glag blustered.

'He's mine! I caught him —— ' Smiggles quailed under the King's glowering eye, '—— from the nest,' he finished lamely.

The King looked at Willi's beaky nose, his flapper-like arms, the strewn feathers. 'From the nest?' he said, and snuffled most unpleasantly. 'Then this thing is a bird. A lyrebird! You can have him, Fox. You can bite his head off.'

'No!' yelled Glag. He grabbed Willi and tried to pull him between the bars. Willi stretched like chewing gum.

'This is one lyrebird what won't ever spoil a Gumble-trap!' the King roared. 'Bite him, Fox!' He was holding the cage in both hands, pressing the wires apart for Fox to put his head in. But Fox hung back, knowing now that those interesting feathers did not belong to Willi, and the King lost all patience and rammed the cage over Fox's head. At the same instant Glag pulled Willi out with a faint plop and dropped him. Toot and Merrigumble rolled him up like a fire hose and took him away for reshaping.

With the cage clamped round his neck, Fox went mad, wild. He thought he was in a trap. He pawed, his jaws snapped and frothed. The Bottersnikes found it the funniest sight they had seen. They waddled into the banqueting hall (where it was safer) and made windows to watch the fun. Finding the cage would not shake off, Fox began to run in short panicky rushes that sent the Bottersnikes into fits of snuffling. The house rocked each time Fox made one of his wild dashes, for the cage was still fastened to the housetop with the plastic rope. The Bottersnikes were enjoying themselves too much to notice this. 'Fox lost his head — what a clown!' they snuffled. 'We oughta keep him as a entertainer.' The funniest part of all, the part that really brought the house down, happened when Fox sat on his haunches and tugged with all his weight. A storm of snuffling went up from the Bottersnikes, the rope snapped — Fox and the cage were free — but the house was already falling.

The bed came down with a crash and a jangle that echoed into the trees. The Bottersnikes thought an earthquake had hit. 'We're buried alive!' they wailed. 'Help, Fox! Come and dig us out.'

But Fox would never come back, never, to a place where he had been trapped and laughed at. He shook free of the cage, and the flash of his red fur as he bounded across the rocks was the last they ever saw of him.

'Fine sort of animal he turned out to be, leavin' his mates buried in the rubble,' the Bottersnikes howled.

The Bottersnikes were not buried alive; there was breathing room for all beneath the big bed though no space to move around. Tink's tink had really come good this time. The Gumbles swiftly rebuilt the side walls, made them quite secure, and put up a roof of palm fronds so that the prisoners would not shrink if it rained.

'We shall have to come back in a week or two and let them out though,' said Willi. He knew what it was like, being penned up.

But even this would not be necessary, they soon saw. For when the Bottersnikes had slimmed down a bit and worked off the effects of their huge banquet they would be able to crawl between the bars at the ends of the bed. In fact if they hadn't eaten so much banquet they wouldn't have been prisoners at all.

The Gumbles began to giggle. *They* were free. They piled all the jam tins they could find into a great pyramid and knocked it down with stones. Old Koala in his gum tree woke at the noise and couldn't for the life of him make out what all the giggling was about. But Gumbles always giggle when they are happy.

Chip-Chip needed no more guarding after that. He grew big enough to leave his nest long before the Bottersnikes grew thin enough to escape from prison; he learned to run, to dig his own worms, to vanish in the fern at the approach of danger. Much later Chip-Chip grew his lyre tail and learned to dance by copying his father. He became great friends with Willigumble especially. He would dance for Willi almost any time except when he was moulting; and when he displayed his two-foot tail, shimmering and silvery and swaying, Willi always thought it was the loveliest thing he had seen.

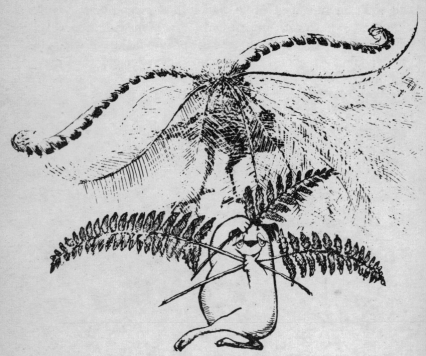

S. A. Wakefield
Bottersnikes and Gumbles £1.25

Deep in the bush live some *very* strange creatures . . . Bottersnikes
have green, wrinkly skin, cheese-grater noses and long, pointed ears
that go red when they're angry (which is most of the time). Gumbles,
on the other hand, are cheerful and friendly and can be squashed into
any shape without being hurt. This was handy for the Bottersnikes,
who, with cries of 'GOT YOU!', grabbed the Gumbles and popped them
into jam tins, ready to be taken out and put to work whenever
anything needed doing around the Bottersnikes rubbish-dump home.
So the battle began. . .

Piccolo fiction you will enjoy

○ **The Fairy Tale Omnibus**		£2.95p
○ **The Keyword and Other Mysteries**	Isaac Asimov	90p
○ **Are you There, God? It's Me, Margaret**		£1.00p
○ **Blubber**		£1.25p
○ **Iggie's House**		£1.00p
○ **Otherwise Known as Sheila the Great**	Judy Blume	£1.00p
○ **Superfudge**		£1.25p
○ **Tales of a Fourth Grade Nothing**		£1.00p
○ **The Mountain of Adventure**	Enid Blyton	£1.00p
○ **The Treasure of Dubarry Castle**	Lindsay Brown	95p
○ **The Secret of the Silver Lockets**		£1.25p
○ **Dolphin Island**	Arthur C. Clarke	£1.25p
○ **The String Family**	Patricia Cleveland-Peck	90p
○ **The String Family in Summer**		95p
○ **The Little Prince**	Antoine de Saint Exupéry	95p
○ **Spring Comes to World's End**	Monica Dickens	35p
○ **Doris Takes a Break**	Hilary Hayton	£1.00p
○ **The Great Ghost Rescue**	Eva Ibbotson	£1.25p
○ **Which Witch?**		£1.25p
○ **Kidnap in Willowbank Wood**	Faith Jaques	£1.50p
○ **The Mouse that Roared**	Ray Jones	90p

○ **The Travels of Oggy**	} Ann Lawrence	95p
○ **Oggy and the Holiday**		90p
○ **The Yearling**	Marjorie Kinnan Rawlings	£1.50p
○ **How to Eat Fried Worms**	Thomas Rockwell	£1.25p
○ **Mr Cogg and His Computer**	Carolyn Sloan	£1.25p
○ **101 Dalmatians**	Dodie Smith	£1.25p
○ **Quincy**	Tommy Steele	95p
○ **Tales of Little Grey Rabbit**	Alison Uttley	£1.25p
○ **The Fastest Gun Alive and Other Night Adventures**	} David Henry Wilson	95p
○ **Elephants Don't Sit on Cars**		95p

All these books are available at your local bookshop or newsagent, or can be ordered direct from the publisher. Indicate the number of copies required and fill in the form below   10

....

Name_____
(Block letters please)

Address_____

_____

Send to CS Department, Pan Books Ltd,
PO Box 40, Basingstoke, Hants
Please enclose remittance to the value of the cover price plus:
35p for the first book plus 15p per copy for each additional book
ordered to a maximum charge of £1.25 to cover postage and
packing
Applicable only in the UK

While every effort is made to keep prices low, it is sometimes
necessary to increase prices at short notice. Pan Books reserve the
right to show on covers and charge new retail prices which may
differ from those advertised in the text or elsewhere